This is a work of fiction. The characters, places, and incidents depicted are entirely a product of the author's imagination. Any resemblance to real persons, living or dead, or actual events is purely coincidental and unintended. The author and publisher bear no responsibility for any perceived similarities.

This novel is dedicated to the innocent souls—boys and girls alike—who suffered unjust punishment under the guise of honour. May their stories never be forgotten, and may justice and compassion prevail.

AUTHOR'S NOTE

In an era where countless stories emerge each day, this novel was not written merely to add to the volume—but to speak to the heart. Across numerous novels, the author has consistently sought to weave emotional and societal threads into narratives that explore justice, love, resilience, and the enduring strength of human connection.

Originally penned in Urdu, these works reflect the rhythms and realities of South Asian life, interwoven with the nuanced experiences of those who navigate the complexities of migration and cultural duality. Their rendering into English marks not just a linguistic shift, but a heartfelt effort to open these stories to a broader audience—inviting understanding across cultures and continents.

Readers from the subcontinent may find echoes of their own lives within these pages, while those in the West are welcomed into a rich tapestry of Eastern traditions, spiritual values, and universal human experiences that transcend borders. I hope these stories spark empathy, reflection, and perhaps even healing—wherever in the world they are read.

DON'T READ ME:

Stories have the power to shape perspectives, to challenge traditions, and to stir the conscience of society. Panah (a word in Urdu language that literally means Refuge) is not merely a tale—it is a mirror reflecting the silent cries of countless voices, lost in the shadows of fear and oppression.

In a world where honour is sometimes mistaken for tyranny, where love is eclipsed by control, and where the right to life is dictated by rigid customs, many dreams are shattered before they are even given the chance to bloom.

This novel is more than fiction—it is a narrative woven with threads of truth, inspired by realities that are often left unspoken. Through the journey of Maiza—a Canadian girl of Pakistani descent, in this novel we witness the defiance of a spirit that refuses to submit to injustice, the desperate search for freedom, and the battle between tradition and humanity.

But this is not just her story—it is a testament to all those who have been silenced, a call for compassion, and a demand for change. Let this tale serve as a reminder—that true honour is found not in oppression, but in the courage to stand against it. The greatest gift parents can offer their children is a well-rounded education, refined manners, respectful conduct, and above all, guidance in righteousness and moral integrity. Sounds too philosophical—I had already said, don't read me! If you are still reading, it's not my fault.

Aakh

"Who are you?"

Rubbing her eyes and pulling her dupatta (scarf) over her head, she asked in English:

"Who are you? And what is this place?"

"What strange language are you speaking? I am asking who you are and how you ended up in my trailer?"

The man uttered in Urdu.

"You are perhaps the lorry driver on whose trailer I hid myself. What is your name?" She was still groggy from sleep. Almost absentmindedly, she murmured again in English.

"You're babbling nonsense again. Speak quickly—who are you and how did you get here?"

The man said in strict tone in distorted Urdu mixed with Pashto language.

Now her senses were returning. She spoke slowly in Urdu, "Do you understand English? I know Urdu but not Pashto at all."

"I understand Urdu. My name is Zordar Khan. I do not know this foreign tongue. Who are you? And how did you get here?" He replied in straight tone which is typical of tribal men.

"So your name is Zordar Khan. Can you help me cross the border?" the girl asked, looking at him.

"You must be out of your mind! I don't even know who you are or how you got here, and you want me to take you across the border? Who are you?" Zordar Khan replied angrily.

"I heard that Pathans are very hospitable. They serve and protect their guests. Can't you help me cross the border?" she asked, looking at Zordar Khan expectantly.

"I could give my life for my guests, but I do not know who you are, what kind of woman you are, or how you ended up here in Landi Kotal [1]. What do you want from me?" Zordar Khan demanded.

"I hid myself in the hay on your trailer and made my way here," she replied.

"Oh God! You must be insane! I have been driving for four hours, and you're telling me you've been hiding in the back of the trailer the entire time? Are you human or what?" Zordar Khan spoke in a mix of astonishment and irritation.

The girl murmured to herself, again in English:

"When you have nothing to lose in life but life itself, then you can do anything..."

"What nonsense are you saying now? I told you before—I do not understand this foreign tongue," Zordar Khan replied irritably.

She took a deep breath and said softly in Urdu, "What I mean is—I am running in search of life. Can you please help me cross the border?"

"You are definitely crazy! Miss, this is tribal territory of Pakistan. FATA! Do you just want to go to Afghanistan from here?" Zordar Khan said in a mixed emotion of anger and confusion.

"I will go anywhere. Please, just get me out of Pakistan!" she pleaded.

"Who are you? What is your name?" Zordar Khan curiously asked.

"Maiza. My name is Maiza. Khan Sahib, please take me to Afghanistan—at least I will be out of Pakistan. Will you help me stay alive? Please," she begged.

"You must have lost your mind! If anyone sees me with you, I will be ruined. Oh God, what kind of trouble have I gotten myself into?" Zordar muttered in frustration.

By now, Maiza had stepped out of the trailer and was brushing off the hay from her clothes. Moving a little closer, she asked, "Can't you help me?"

Zordar Khan quickly stepped back and barked, "What kind of shameless woman are you? Speak from a distance! First, you don't cover yourself properly, and second, you deceitfully hid in my trailer and made it all the way here. What do you want?"

"I just don't want to die yet—I want to escape," she said in a strange tone.

"Are you not afraid—wandering alone, arriving in an unknown place?" Zordar Khan asked in a voice filled with disbelief.

"Not anymore. Tell me—will you help me?" she asked, looking at him expectantly.

"I can't do anything. Just leave my field and land, and then go wherever you want!" Zordar replied impatiently.

"Where should I go? At least show me the way out of here!" Maiza said, her tone growing despondent.

"Yes, absolutely. Leave, because if anyone sees me with you, I will be in deep trouble. My reputation will be ruined! Just go!" Zordar Khan insisted.

Hearing this, Maiza snapped irritably, "Fine! I'm leaving. But at least show me the way out!"

Zordar Khan gestured toward a path and said, "See that foot trail? Just walk straight along it—you'll exit my land and fields. After that, go wherever you want. I don't care."

She hesitated for a moment before speaking again, "Okay, I'll go. But please, can I have some water?"

Zordar Khan paused for a moment, then fetched a pitcher and a glass and placed them on the bonnet of his pickup truck.

Maiza drank the water hastily, as if she had been parched for days. After finishing, she set the glass down and said in a firm voice, "Thank you."

Then, she walked toward the foot trail.

After Maiza left, Zordar Khan busied himself with work in his fields, but his mind remained tangled in the unexpected actions and strange words of the girl.

After working for an hour, he thought to himself, time of the Maghrib prayer is approaching—I should return to the village.

So, he gathered his tools, climbed into his pickup, and began driving along the dirt road beside the footpath.

Just as he exited his fields, he noticed the girl sitting on the ground a little ahead—right where the footpath ended.

Zordar Khan kept driving for a short distance, but his eyes frequently glanced at her in the rear-view mirror.

Finally, he stopped the vehicle, reversed it, and stepped out. Approaching her, he asked:

"What are you doing here? Why haven't you left?"

Maiza lifted her head and said with slight irritation, "Why? Is this your land too?"

He looked a little embarrassed. "No, it isn't mine. But why are you sitting here on the ground?"

"Why does that concern you?" she snapped.

"I don't mean anything by it, but Maghrib is near—it's going to get dark. There are wild animals here. Aren't you afraid? You're a strange woman," Zordar said in tribal accent with bewilderment.

"You didn't offer me shelter. You refused hospitality. When I asked for help, you outrightly rejected me. So what have you come here for now? Just go," she said angrily, turning her face away.

"Oh God… What kind of peculiar woman are you? You don't even get scared. Do you not fear for your life and honour, running away from home like this and ending up here all alone?" He rubbed his temples in exasperation.

"I value for my honour greatly," she murmured. "But my fear of death was so overwhelming that I ran without worrying about anything else."

"Now, if you won't help me cross the border, then go away and leave me to sit here in peace," she said firmly.

Hearing this, Zordar Khan looked concerned. "It's getting dark, and there are wild animals here."

She looked at him and said, "So what? The wild animals will tear me apart. But that death is better than the humiliation and obscurity I ran away from."

"You've put me in a tough spot," he sighed. "Alright—get into the pickup."

Maiza brightened. "Really? Will you help me cross the border?"

"It's already night, and there is no light on the roads. I will take you tomorrow. For now, come with me to my house," Zordar Khan said.

Standing up, Maiza asked in surprise, "To your house? Why?"

Zordar Khan responded angrily: "Then where else should I take you at this hour? You've put me in serious trouble. I have no idea what my family will say. I hope this doesn't ruin me!"

Maiza glanced at him and walked to the pickup, opening the front door to sit down.

But suddenly, Zordar Khan yelled, "What are you doing?!"

Startled, Maiza looked at him, confused. "You just told me to come with you!"

"Yes, I did. But not on the front seat—sit in the back! What kind of woman are you?! Have you no shame? And cover yourself properly—if anyone sees you like this, it'll bring a whole new kind of trouble upon me. Here, take my shawl and use it for cover." He said, handing her his shawl.

Maiza was already cold, so she quickly wrapped herself in the shawl and climbed into the back seat.

AUTHOR'S NOTE:

Landi Kotal, nestled in the rugged terrain of Khyber Pakhtunkhwa Province of Pakistan, is a town of historical and cultural significance. It was once part of the Federally Administered Tribal Areas (FATA) before the region merged with Khyber Pakhtunkhwa in 2018.

Landi Kotal town is located near the Torkham border which serves as a trade route between Pakistan and Afghanistan. The town is predominantly inhabited by Pashtun tribes. Islam is the dominant religion in Landi Kotal. The town is deeply rooted in Pashtun traditions, which emphasize hospitality, honour, and tribal loyalty. The Pashto language is widely spoken, and traditional Pashtun attire, including shalwar kameez and turbans, is commonly worn by men. Women traditionally observe purdah, limiting their interactions with men outside their family and wearing modest attire.

On the way, Zordar Khan said, "I am bound by my traditions. You drank water on my land. Whoever seeks refuge and hospitality from me on my land—I cannot refuse them. But bringing a strange woman into my village and home—that is not our tradition either. I feel like I am about to face serious trouble."

"Then just take me straight to the border!" Maiza called from the back.

Zordar Khan snapped, "You are a strange woman! It's night-time already—there's no light, and the Torkham border is four hours ahead. Then Kabul is another two hours from there. I cannot take you now."

"Then what will you tell your family?" Maiza asked after a moment of thought.

"That's exactly what I'm worried about. I have never lied before, but now, because of you, I might have to make something up," Zordar Khan said with concern.

The pickup rattled along the uneven dirt path, dust rising in golden streaks under the afternoon sun. The vast expanse of rugged hills stretched endlessly ahead, their silence heavier than the burden weighing on Zordar Khan's chest. In the back, Maiza, wrapped in his shawl, remained quiet, staring out into nothingness.

"What have I done?" Zordar thought to himself, gripping the wheel tighter.

Bringing a strange woman into his home—defying tradition, risking disgrace. He had been taught that a man's name was his honour, and yet here he was, carrying a foreign woman across tribal lands, knowing full well that eyes would watch, tongues would wag.

"This is madness," he muttered under his breath.

But a counter-thought rose—what choice did she have? What choice did he have, when the weight of his own conscience demanded action?

"You look troubled," Maiza remarked, her voice gentle but probing.

Zordar glanced at her in the back-view mirror, and for a fleeting moment, he considered confessing the turmoil clawing at his heart. But instead, he scoffed, waving it off.

After driving through rough and uneven roads, the pickup truck entered a village about half an hour later. The sun had set, and darkness had spread over the land. There was barely any light—only a few bulbs flickered in some houses, and an eerie silence blanketed everything.

After navigating the village streets for a while, the pickup truck finally pulled into a house.

Zordar Khan parked the vehicle inside and turned to Maiza. "Stay in the pickup for now. I'll be back soon," he said before heading inside.

Maiza sat in the pickup, lost in thought.

A little while later, Zordar Khan returned, accompanied by a girl around Maiza's age. She wore a large shawl draped over her head.

Standing apart from them, Zordar Khan addressed the girl, "Faiza Khani, take her to the women's quarters. She is a guest. She will stay here tonight. Tomorrow at noon, I will take her to her family in Kabul."

Faiza looked at Zordar Khan with curiosity but said nothing.

She then approached Maiza and said, "Assalam o Alaikum. Come with me, I'll take you to the guest room."

Maiza climbed out of the pickup, stealing a glance at Zordar Khan, who had turned his face away and stood at a slight distance.

Then, she followed Faiza into the house.

"What do you mean?! Zordar brought a woman here? What are you saying?"

"Yes, Mother, I am telling the truth. I just left the girl in the guest room," Faiza replied.

"I cannot believe it! Zordar is not that kind of man. Who is this woman?"

Zordar Khan's mother curiously asked.

"Brother said she is the sister of a friend of his. She got separated from her family in Peshawar, so he brought her here. Tomorrow, he will take her to her family in Kabul," Faiza explained.

"What kind of story is this? What is going on? And when did he get a new friend from Kabul? My God! He brought this strange woman all the way from Peshawar to here, alone? If people find out about this, they will spread all kinds of rumours. And what will I tell your father?"

Zordar Khan's mother said in distress.

Faiza, growing worried, asked, "Now what should we do?"

"Listen, for now, do not speak about this to anyone, and don't tell anyone anything. Go call Zordar—I will talk to him myself. Actually, wait—first, let's go meet the woman in the guest room," she said.

When they arrived at the guest room, Maiza had already freshened up.

Seeing Faiza enter with an older woman, she realized it must be Zordar's mother.

She stood up, greeted her with salam, and extended her hand for a handshake.

Zordar's mother scanned her from head to toe before returning the greeting and asking, "What is your name? Where is your family?"

"My name is Maiza. My family was separated from me in Peshawar, and I want to go to them in Kabul."

Maiza told her the same story that Zordar Khan had instructed her to say.

"If you are from Kabul, what were you doing in Peshawar? By the way, you don't look like you're from Kabul—neither by appearance nor by the way you dress," Zordar's mother said, eyeing her suspiciously.

Maiza was caught off guard, unsure how to respond. Nervously, she said, "I am very tired."

Then, unintentionally, she murmured in English,

"Can I take rest now? Talk to you tomorrow..."

But she realized her mistake immediately and quickly corrected herself and said in Urdu, "I—I'm sorry. I meant to say, if you don't mind, I would like to rest now, and we can talk tomorrow."

Zordar's mother studied her carefully before saying, "Fine. Rest now. We will talk tomorrow."

Then, she took Faiza's hand and left the room.

Once they were gone, Maiza let out a deep breath of relief and sat on the bed.

After stepping outside, Zordar's mother walked a little way with Faiza and said, "She seems like a city girl to me. Didn't you notice how fluently she spoke that foreign language? I think Zordar is hiding something."

"Yes, Mother, I feel the same way," Faiza agreed.

Zordar's mother leaned in conspiratorially, "Listen carefully to what I'm saying. We must tell everyone that she is the sister of Zordar's close friend. Her family had to leave urgently for Kabul, so they left her with us. Do not say that Zordar brought her here himself!"

Faiza looked curiously at her mother.

"We must tell everyone that she is a guest, and that her family will come to take her soon—or we will take her to them in Kabul ourselves. This is necessary to avoid disgrace and trouble. Do you understand? You must say exactly what I have told you." Zordar's mother instructed her daughter.

"Yes, Mother, I'll say that," Faiza replied in anxious voice.

"And where is Zordar? Send him to me!" his mother instructed.

"Mother, I told you—she was separated from her family in Peshawar. Tomorrow, I will take her to Kabul. It's just for one night," Zordar Khan explained.

"I do not believe you," his mother said, her face filled with suspicion and frustration. "And don't you know our traditions?"

"I do, Mother. But what could I do? I was forced into this situation," Zordar Khan said, shrugging his shoulders.

"Do you think I grew these grey hairs under the sun for nothing?" she asked, glaring at him.

"I don't understand what you mean."

Zordar Khan replied.

"What is this 'compulsion' you speak of? How and where did you meet this girl?"

she asked, her voice dripping with doubt.

"Mother, it's a long story. I'll tell you later. Right now, just give her some food. I'm exhausted—I need rest. I'll talk to you in the morning," Zordar Khan said, quickly bidding her farewell before slipping away.

That night, when Zordar's father returned from a tribal gathering, his wife informed him, "She is our guest. Her family will soon come to take her, or we will take her to Kabul ourselves. I personally gave Zordar permission for his friend's family to leave her with us," she said, watching her husband's reaction carefully.

Hearing this, Zordar's father replied, "Yes, yes, why not? She is our guest. Let her stay as long as she wants. Take care of her. Now tell me—where is Zordar? Did he bring everything back from Peshawar?"

She breathed a sigh of relief—at least her husband had not raised any objections or suspicions.

"Yes, he brought everything back. But he was tired, so he went to sleep," she replied.

The next morning, Zordar Khan said to Faiza, "Give the guest a burqa (a traditional cover-all) and tell her to get ready. We will leave for Kabul at ten o'clock. You get ready too—you're coming with us."

At ten o'clock, the three of them set off in the pickup.

Faiza sat next to her brother in the front seat, while Maiza was in the back.

After traveling a short distance, a thought struck Zordar Khan. He turned to Maiza and asked, "You have your passport, right?"

"No, I don't have a passport," Maiza replied.

"What?! You don't have one?!" Zordar Khan exclaimed in shock. "Then you must have an ID card at least?"

"I don't have that either," Maiza replied simply.

"What?! You don't have that either?"

At this, Zordar Khan slammed on the brakes so suddenly that Faiza nearly hit the windshield, and Maiza was jolted forward, tumbling onto Faiza's seat.

His anger skyrocketed. He yelled, "If you don't have any identification documents, how do you expect me to get you across the Torkham border?! Are you crazy? Why didn't you tell me earlier?!"

"You never asked," Maiza replied matter-of-factly.

"Oh God… Is this some kind of joke?!" Zordar Khan said, fuming.

Faiza turned to Maiza and asked, "Maiza, where is your ID card and passport? We can go back to get them and then take you to Kabul."

Maiza hesitated, as if she wanted to say something but held back. Then she said, "Actually… instead, take me to Islamabad."

Faiza and Zordar Khan stared at her as if she had just descended from another planet.

"Do you even realize how far Islamabad is from here? And do you know the kind of problems we'll face on the way?"

Zordar Khan asked, his frustration evident.

Maiza shook her head. "I don't know anything about this place. I only know that if you take me to the Canadian embassy in Islamabad, I might be able to figure things out."

Zordar Khan's anger reached its peak.

"Islamabad is about a five-hour drive from here. There are strict security checks along the way. You must be insane! First, you ask me to take you to Kabul—now you want me to take you to Islamabad?! What exactly do you want?!"

Faiza stared at Maiza in shock, wondering what exactly was going on.

Maiza said, "I am very sorry. I have troubled you all too much. Since it's daytime, I'll get off here, find my own way, and somehow reach Islamabad."

With that, she stepped out of the pickup.

Faiza quickly followed, grabbing her hand and saying, "No, Maiza! Please don't say that. We cannot leave you alone like this."

Seeing all this, Zordar Khan's anger began to subside.

He also stepped out of the pickup and spoke calmly, "Faiza Khani is right. You are under my protection—it is my responsibility. I cannot leave you alone here, but I also cannot take you to Islamabad right away. I need to prepare for the journey."

Faiza looked at Zordar Khan and said, "Brother, may I give you a suggestion?"

"Go ahead. My brain is already fried," Zordar Khan muttered.

"Brother, let's take Maiza back home for now. I will speak to Mother myself. Meanwhile, you can make arrangements for the trip. Once everything is set, we will take her to Islamabad," she suggested.

"No, Faiza, please let it be. I have already caused too much trouble for you all. You should go back—I will figure things out myself."

Maiza said firmly.

"I cannot leave you here like this. Faiza Khani is right. For now, you will come back home with us. I will prepare for the journey and then take you to Islamabad."

Zordar Khan declared.

"Yes, Maiza, don't be stubborn. Come with us please," Faiza said, helping her back into the pickup.

"You two brought her back again?!"

"Now what will happen?" Zordar Khan's mother said, looking at Faiza.

When Faiza explained everything, she grew even more anxious. "I am afraid that this might create a new problem. You know your aunt and some of the women in the family—they blow every small thing out of proportion. If they find out about this, they will spread all kinds of rumours."

Faiza, equally worried, responded, "Yes, Mother, it is a concerning situation. But how could we leave her alone there? What do we do now?"

Her mother sighed, "Tell me—why does she suddenly want to go to Islamabad?"

"Mother, I don't know. Honestly, sometimes her words seem very strange to me," Faiza admitted.

"Why doesn't she just call her family to come and get her?" her mother asked.

"I don't know the real reason, Mother," Faiza said uneasily.

"Daughter, do one thing—go to her, and casually try to figure out the truth behind all this. Could this be some sort of conspiracy from our enemies? I am very worried," her mother said.

"Mother, I feel something is off too. When Brother got angry with her and said, 'You don't have any identification documents—how can we take you to Kabul?' she suddenly got out of the pickup and said she would go to Islamabad alone."

" Oh!!! " Zordar's mother exclaimed.

"If she really is the sister of Brother's friend, why did she do that? And why is she saying such things?" Faiza said, her voice filled with doubt.

"Khocha, one milk tea and a paratha!"

Zordar Khan called out in Pashto -Urdu mixed accent, as he sat down at a roadside tea stall. His mind was in turmoil—he couldn't figure out what to do or how to help the girl reach her destination.

Lost in his thoughts, he barely noticed when a boy arrived with a small kettle of tea and a plate of paratha, placing the tray in front of him.

Zordar Khan poured the tea into a cup and started eating the paratha, which was resting on a piece of newspaper.

Suddenly, his eyes landed on the newspaper fragment. His hands trembled, almost dropping the cup.

"Oh God! What is this?"

The torn newspaper piece contained a picture of Maiza—alongside an article.

Zordar Khan couldn't read Urdu, so he had no idea what the article said. But instinctively, he folded the newspaper scrap carefully and tucked it into his pocket.

Finishing his tea hastily, he left the stall in a rush.

"Faiza Khani, come here. I need your help with something important," Zordar Khan called her in a low, serious tone.

"Yes, brother, what is it?" Faiza asked as she approached him.

"I'll explain, but first, tell me—Mother isn't angry, is she?" he asked nervously.

"Brother, she's not just angry—she's extremely worried. She told me not to let any of our younger sisters go near Maiza," Faiza responded.

Before she could continue, Zordar Khan signalled her to stop. Then, in secret, he pulled out the newspaper fragment with Maiza's picture and handed it to her.

"Look at this. Her picture is in the newspaper! You can read—tell me what it says!"

Faiza examined the image and read the news.

"Brother… what is going on?" she worriedly murmured.

"What do you mean? Hurry up and tell me what's written!" Zordar Khan asked, his voice full of anxiety.

"Brother, the article says that Maiza is dead. Some people claim she was murdered by her own family in an 'honour killing.' The second thing is—she has been lying to us about her name. The article states that her real name is Laiza, and that she is a Canadian of Pakistani descent," Faiza perplexedly said.

"Yara, what are you saying?" Zordar Khan muttered.

"I don't understand any of this. If she's dead, then who has been lying to me? And if she's lying, then who actually died?! Oh God… is she a ghost? Faiza Khani, have you ever touched her?" he asked hesitantly.

"N-No, brother… I feel very uneasy. I'm scared," Faiza whispered, her fear evident.

"There's no need to be scared. I'm still alive. But what is this 'Ka-ne-da'? What sort of place is it, and why does she want to go there?"

Zordar Khan asked in confusion.

"Brother, Canada is not some strange creature—it is a country. Like Pakistan, Afghanistan, and Iran, Canada is also a nation. It is very far from here," Faiza explained.

"Alright, anyway do one thing—go to the guest room and touch her. See if she is actually human or some kind of spirit," Zordar Khan instructed.

"N-No, brother! I won't go!" Faiza refused in a trembling voice.

"Don't be afraid—I'll be right outside. If anything feels wrong, call me—I'll come immediately," he tried to reassure her.

"No, brother! I won't go! What if she is a ghost and clings to me?" Faiza said, terrified.

"Don't be scared. Nothing will happen. I'll be outside—just go in," he insisted, gently pushing her toward the guest room.

Faiza stumbled inside hesitantly.

Maiza was seated on a chair, lost in deep thought.

When she saw Faiza enter so abruptly, she stood up.

Faiza was startled—her breath hitched, and she stumbled back in fear.

Seeing her sudden reaction, Maiza asked, "What's wrong?"

She stepped toward Faiza, who froze in terror, her face turning pale.

She tried to back away but lost her balance and fell to the floor.

Fear gripped her so tightly that she couldn't even scream—although she desperately wanted to call for her brother. Her body trembled as panic took hold of her.

Maiza quickly approached, helped Faiza up, and sat her down on the chair.

"Faiza, are you okay? Your face is turning yellow. What happened?"

Feeling the warmth of Maiza's hand, Faiza relaxed slightly.

She realized Maiza wasn't a ghost—she was human.

Still, she remained deeply unsettled.

Noticing Faiza's fearful state, Maiza said, "Why are you so frightened? You look scared. Are you uncomfortable because I arrived uninvited? "

Faiza was still speechless.

Maiza said, "If so, you have a fair point. But please, just endure my presence for another day or two—then I will leave. Escaping the messengers of death in search of life is no easy task."

"W-What do you mean? I don't understand," Faiza asked cautiously.

"The truth is… death is chasing me. But I want to live," Maiza said in an eerie tone.

Outside, when Zordar Khan heard no cries for help, his suspicions deepened.

Standing near the room's entrance, he coughed loudly.

Inside, Faiza understood—he was checking whether she was alright. She turned to Maiza and said, "Wait a moment. I'll be right back."

She stepped outside and whispered to Zordar Khan, "Brother, she is human—alive. It seems the newspaper article was wrong."

"But I don't understand… the picture is clearly hers."

Zordar Khan perplexedly said.

Faiza shrugged her shoulders and said, "Anyway, you should leave now. I will go back in and try to learn the truth from her."

The night was still, except for the distant howls of wild dogs echoing across the rugged landscape. Zordar Khan stood outside his home, staring at the dark horizon, uncertainty clawing at his chest. He exhaled sharply, then turned toward the small clay-walled house of Haji Usman—the village elder known for his wisdom.

Inside, the flickering light of an oil lamp cast long shadows as Usman sipped his tea. He looked up as Zordar entered, his heavy steps betraying an unspoken burden.

"What troubles you, Son?" the old man asked, setting his tea aside.

Zordar hesitated, rubbing his temples.

"I have taken in a woman. A stranger, running from something worse than death. But my honour—my family's name—is at stake."

Usman leaned forward, his weathered face thoughtful.

"Tell me, does your heart say she is innocent?"

Zordar swallowed.

"I don't know who she is. But I know fear when I see it. And hers is not the fear of deception—it is the fear of the hunted."

Usman sighed, stroking his white beard.

"Our traditions demand caution. Yet, our faith demands justice. You must decide which burden weighs heavier on your soul."

Zordar lowered his gaze. He had always followed the laws of his land. But now, those laws conflicted with his conscience.

"If I do nothing, she may die," he murmured.

"Then perhaps it is time for our traditions to be tested," Usman replied, his voice firm.

Maiza spoke as she saw Faiza enter the room again, "What happened, is everything alright?"

"Yes, everything is fine. You were saying that someone is after you and wants to kill you. But why?" Faiza asked after sitting down.

"Death is chasing me, but I have made a decision—I will not surrender myself so easily." Maiza replied mysteriously.

Faiza listened carefully and then cautiously placed a newspaper clipping in front of her, gazing at her with questioning eyes.

Maiza picked up the clipping, examined it, and asked, "Where did you get this?" Then, noticing Faiza's silent but inquisitive expression, she said, "Are you mistaking me for Laiza?"

When Faiza slowly nodded in affirmation, Maiza continued, "Yes, it's true that my sister and I looked very similar. But Laiza was a year older than me. My innocent sister was murdered by those people."

Saying this, Maiza broke down into tears.

After a while, when she regained her composure, she said, "But I decided that unlike Laiza, I would not embrace death in silence."

"How was your sister killed? Who murdered her?" Faiza hesitated before asking.

Maiza replied, "The ones who killed her were not strangers but rather our own—so close that you wouldn't even imagine such a betrayal. They claimed she died a natural death, but I know she was murdered. Her burial was carried out quietly in the night, and the matter was suppressed."

Faiza looked at her and asked, "Oh... Then what happened?"

Maiza continued, "She had a very close friend in Canada. When the news of Laiza's sudden passing reached her, she couldn't believe it. Since she was somewhat aware of our shattered family affairs, she pushed for the news to be published in the local newspapers, hoping for some action. However, the police here barely conducted a superficial inquiry, and the case was silenced. The one who left will never return, but the injustice committed against her haunts me every night."

As she said this, Maiza wiped her tears.

Faiza sighed with sympathy and said, "Listening to your story truly saddens me. Are you Canadian?"

"Yes, we are Canadians of Pakistani descent." Then, looking at Faiza, Maiza said, "You seem educated—not like your brother."

Faiza smiled lightly and responded, "Yes, I have studied till high school. But further education is neither common here nor are there many opportunities."

She was about to say more when she heard someone calling her from outside.

"I think mother is calling me. I should go. You should rest. I'll come again." Faiza said before leaving.

As Faiza entered her mother's room, she was immediately asked, "What was she saying?"

"Mother, I think she is in serious trouble. We need to help her," Faiza replied.

"But what does Zordar have to do with this girl?" her mother asked.

"Mother, everyone was wrong. She is not the sister of any of my brother's friends. In fact, my brother barely knows her. I think she must have crossed paths with him while fleeing for her life. She's not even Pakistani—she's Canadian of Pakistani origin. "

Faiza explained.

"Oh… Now I am really worried about what I will tell your aunt, your uncle's wife, and the other women who are coming here for breakfast tomorrow morning. If they see this girl here, I don't know what kind of storm they will create. They turn even the smallest matters into scandals. May God protect us," her mother spoke with anxiety.

"Mother, it's not possible to send her to Islamabad so quickly. Brother said he can't take her in his pickup. Also, may God ruin the heartless foreign powers and their allies—they keep bombing us, launching drone attacks, killing thousands of innocent people, and labelling us terrorists before the world. They have imposed restrictions on us."

Faiza worriedly said.

" What do you mean by this?"

Her mother confusedly enquired.

" They caught a few conspirators among us, and now they see the entire tribal population as criminals and wrongdoers. That is why my brother is worried about traveling to the capital—security checks on our people along the way are extremely strict," Faiza explained.

"Then what will happen now? What will we tell those women?" her mother asked, her voice filled with worry.

"Mother, don't worry. I will explain everything to Maiza and tell her to remain completely silent in front of the women. Even if they ask something, she should respond vaguely or say nothing at all," Faiza assured her mother.

"Yes, my dear… go and make sure she understands properly. May God protect us," her mother replied, but her tone still reflected her deep concern.

Phuppi (paternal aunt) Jameela, Khala (maternal aunt) Noreen, and a group of other women made up a clique of troublemakers in the family. They were notorious for spreading rumours, gossiping, mocking others, and stirring up chaos. The entire family was tired and fearful of their antics, but since they were relatives, people tolerated them.

When they saw an unfamiliar girl in the guest room, despite all the explanations given by Zordar's mother and sister, they refused to believe anything and started whispering among themselves:

"Something is definitely wrong. It's unheard of for a young girl to suddenly lose contact with her family, and yet they haven't come to take her back. They are hiding something from us."

Faiza tried to explained:

"No, Khala Noreen, there's nothing like that. We are not hiding anything from you."

Hearing this, her Phuppi Jameela snapped:

"You should stay quiet. Let us ask Zarmina—how shocking! A house full of daughters, yet a completely unrelated young girl is living here without any connection or bond. May God protect us. The final hour has arrived. What kind of times have we come to?"

The women continued their chatter and eventually left. After they were gone, Faiza spoke anxiously:

Mother, what will we do now? They didn't believe a single word we said."

"I knew it! Zordar will be the reason for our disgrace. He won't leave us with any dignity," her mother fumed as she stood up, grabbed Faiza's hand, and said, "Come with me. First thing in the morning, we will get rid of this girl. Before she becomes a mark of disgrace for us, we must send her away."

Faiza pulled her hand away, saying, "Mother, wait! Acting too hastily isn't wise. At least talk to brother first."

"What's the point in asking that useless boy? He has no regard for our honour and traditions," her mother retorted angrily.

"Even so, Mother, speak to him at least once. Otherwise, he will be furious," Faiza insisted nervously.

"Fine! But today, everything must be made clear. Go now and bring that useless Zordar here," her mother commanded in frustration.

"Mother, brother is out somewhere. I will send him to you as soon as he returns," Faiza replied.

The whispers began subtly, like wind brushing through dry leaves. Then they grew louder, spreading from house to house, gathering weight with every retelling.

By the afternoon, two elderly men sat outside the tea shop, discussing the matter.

"Have you heard? Zordar Khan has taken in a woman. No one knows where she came from."

"And he expects the village to remain silent?" the other scoffed.

Nearby, a group of women exchanged glances, their voices hushed.

"Who knows what kind of woman she is?" one murmured. "A respectable girl does not go to live like this in stranger's home."

The words dripped with disapproval.

In parallel, inside the family gathering space, Zordar's Phuppi Jameela and Khala Noreen, sat with several women from the village, her voice filled with accusation.

"This is unacceptable, Zordar has brought a strange woman into his home? How ridiculous is this!" Khala Noreen said.

Phuppi Jameela spread more poison, "This is extremely immoral and against our religion practices and tribal norms."

"Yara, I need a clean Jeep. I have to take my family to Islamabad," Zordar Khan said.

"Zordar Khan, you've never taken your family out of Khyber Agency before. Why are you suddenly going to Islamabad?" his friend curiously asked.

"It's an urgent matter. I will explain later. Tell me—can I get a new-model Jeep with proper documents? You know I can't take my pickup because its number plate is fake. The security checks in Islamabad are tough, and I don't want to get caught," Zordar Khan explained.

"I don't understand why you need to go there so suddenly. Zordar Khan, you know we only have a small Jeep, but that won't be suitable. Give me a little time—I have a friend in Peshawar who owns a new-model Land Cruiser Prado. I'll speak to him," his friend offered.

"Mahmood Afridi, you are my brother. Please find a way to arrange this. Whatever rent your friend asks, I'll pay. I'll also use the Jeep carefully," Zordar Khan said.

"Alright, don't worry. I'll talk to him today itself," his friend replied.

Faiza entered the guest room and found Maiza sitting on a chair, gazing blankly out of the window. As she noticed Faiza, she spoke softly, "Come in, Faiza..."

"I brought some tea for you," Faiza said, placing the tray on the table. She removed the tea cozy, poured a cup, and extended it toward Maiza.

Smiling as she took the cup, Maiza said, "Thank you, you people are very kind and hospitable."

"May I ask you a question?" Faiza asked, looking at her.

"Of course," Maiza replied while sipping her tea.

"Are your own family members the ones trying to harm you?" Faiza asked.

"Yes, it's true. When one's own home becomes a slaughterhouse, and the very protectors turn into murderers... there is no refuge left," Maiza responded with a deep sadness in her tone.

"But how did it come to this? I mean, how did you end up in such circumstances?" Faiza asked.

Maiza began her story:

"It's a long and painful tale. There were two of us—my sister, Laiza, was a year older than me. She was born in Pakistan. A few months after her birth, my parents obtained Canadian immigration and moved there. I was born in Edmonton. Our childhood was spent in Canada. My father was a banker and held a high position at a private bank. Financially, we were very well off.

When my sister and I started school, my mother found herself with free time at home. So, she began social work, taking a part-time job at a community centre.

Eventually, it turned into a full-time role, and she was appointed head of the social outreach program. She became so engrossed in her work that she forgot she had two young daughters at home, longing for her attention and love.

Every Sunday, my father would take us to an Islamic school held at a mosque. He would drop us off and go shopping or on outings with my mother. When he came to pick us up, it would usually be around Asr prayer time, but he never felt inclined to step inside and pray in congregation. Instead, he would simply collect us and leave.

The teachers at the Islamic school emphasized prayer, but Laiza and I would often think—our parents themselves do not pray regularly, yet they send us here to listen to sermons. They do not practice Islam, yet they insist we attend Islamic school.

Fridays were working days in Canada, so we weren't sure, but we assumed our father might occasionally go for Friday prayers. Other than that, we never saw him visiting the mosque. The Quran—what it was, how it was recited—was something unfamiliar to us. We had seen it placed on a shelf in the cupboard, but we had never seen our parents pick it up, let alone read it.

My mother dressed in modern Western clothing, just like the people she worked with—men and women alike. The Holy month of Ramadan would come and go, but there were no noticeable changes in our household routines.

My father valued his career above all else. His obsession was earning more and more money, climbing the ladder of success. He kept advancing, securing higher positions, and we moved into larger, more luxurious homes. But amidst all this, he neglected his family and failed to provide the necessary guidance.

He assumed that taking us to Sunday Islamic school was like a magic wand—something that would automatically shape us into practicing pious Muslims. To him, the responsibility ended there, shifting to the teachers at the school.

His relentless pursuit of wealth left no room for family time. He thought providing us with the best clothes and comforts was enough. In the process, he forgot that while he had given us worldly luxuries, he had deprived us of a father's affection, attention, and moral upbringing.

Laiza and I were constantly caught in a battle between right and wrong. The lack of parental attention, coupled with the environment at school, threw our minds and personalities into turmoil. I cannot deny that those schools subtly encourage children toward ingratitude, immodesty, selfishness, and even atheism. Education there is free, but it comes with invisible influences—values that seep into young minds, shaping perspectives in ways that families like ours struggle to comprehend.

Faiza, you can imagine the kind of mental chaos we suffered.

On one hand, the distinction between right and wrong was becoming blurry, and on the other, the hypocrisy at home was pushing us toward rebellion. Over time, we started to drift away from Islam—an unconscious opposition and defiance crept into our hearts. The open culture, boundless freedom—these things began to appeal to us. The revealing clothes and bold styles of Western girls fascinated us. The concept of boys and girls freely mingling, dating openly—it seemed normal, even desirable. Watching our classmates embrace fashion trends and form friendships with boys, we too gradually found ourselves walking the same path.

But just as our journey had barely begun, one day, Laiza's boyfriend came to pick her up from home. Coincidentally, my father was at home that day, and Laiza wasn't aware of it. When my father saw her leaving on the back of his motorcycle, everything changed. For the first time in years, his dormant sense of honour and religious conscience awakened.

When Laiza returned home that evening, he scolded her harshly, issuing a stern warning that such a thing must never happen again. From that day forward, he imposed strict rules upon us—we were now required to wear an abaya and hijab whenever we stepped outside.

Upon hearing this, we both looked toward our mother, who had spent her entire youth in Canada without ever covering herself, always wearing fashionable Western clothes. My father then commanded, in a firm and authoritative tone, "From today, she will also wear the hijab and abaya." And so, unwillingly, she too began to observe purdah.

One day, I was about to step outside without a hijab when my mother stopped me, "Maiza, what are you doing? Your father will be furious. Go put on an abaya and hijab before leaving."

I was already fed up with these restrictions. In anger, I responded, "You enjoyed your youth freely, dressed in style, embraced fashion—now you've adopted purdah in old age. Let me live my life with freedom, too! My college friends mock me. They say, 'What happened to you? Why are you suddenly covered up all the time?' I am tired of being ridiculed daily. One by one, all my friends are distancing themselves from me."

My mother angrily uttered: " Don't give me justification. "

"I will not wear an abaya or hijab!" I declared stubbornly and left the house just as I was.

That evening, when I returned home, my father was waiting for me inside. The moment I entered, he slapped me twice and said angrily, "If you don't stop this behaviour, I will forbid you from going to college."

I was infuriated and replied through tears, "You can't oppress me like this! I will call 911."

The moment he heard this, he fell completely silent. His fury evaporated instantly, and without saying another word, he walked away.

I stood there for a long time, clutching my cheek, letting my tears fall. My mother remained quiet, watching everything unfold. But Laiza took me to my room, scolding and urging me to stop being so rebellious.

Still crying, I told Laiza, "They don't pray themselves, yet they expect us to. They've never even touched the Quran, yet they order us to read it daily. Mother spent her whole life without purdah, yet now she forces it upon us. When she worked in social services, she freely interacted with men, attended parties—none of that was wrong then. But now, suddenly, we are forbidden to talk to boys because they are non-mahram (unrelated). I can't bear this hypocrisy!"

Laiza pulled me into an embrace, wiped my tears, and said, "I am tired of this double standard, too. Life isn't a remote control that you can leave in free mode one moment and then suddenly switch to Islamic mode the next. If our parents truly cared about religion, they should have been our role models from the start. If, after all these years, they have realized their mistakes and genuinely wish to follow Islam, they should at least give us time to accept it with sincerity—not through force and coercion. I don't know what to do."

Nevertheless, from that day on, we stopped defying our father's commands, and he, in turn, eased his strictness and control. One day, Father came home while both of us sisters were sitting in the lounge. Speaking loudly to Mother, he said, "My childhood best friend's son is getting married in Pakistan, and he dearly wishes for me to attend with my family. It's a great opportunity to meet our relatives too—it's been a long time since we've seen them."

We didn't pay much attention to his words because, in our entire lives, we had only visited Pakistan once, as Father never liked going there. We thought, "It's good—Mother and Father will go to the wedding, and we'll stay here peacefully."

Soon, both of them became engrossed in making plans for the wedding. Then, one night, they gathered us all and announced, "Next Sunday, we're going to Peshawar for a week. We'll attend the wedding ceremonies and return immediately."

Laiza objected, saying, "I have exams coming up—I can't go." I also refused, saying, "I have no interest in going to Peshawar or attending a wedding in Pakistan."

But Mother insisted, "It's only for a week." We responded, "You both go and attend the wedding." But they pressured us relentlessly. After much resistance, we finally agreed, thinking, "It's just a week—like a short imprisonment. We'll endure it."

Little did we know that what we considered a one-week prison sentence would turn into a lifelong nightmare—a torment without escape. For my beloved sister, that prison did not remain just life imprisonment—it was converted into a death sentence.

"Oh, my sister...!" Overcome with grief, Maiza began sobbing uncontrollably.

Faiza's eyes also welled up with tears.

She handed Maiza a tissue and a glass of water. After drinking some water and composing herself, Maiza continued:

"When we arrived in Pakistan, our parents' behaviour completely changed. They treated us with unbearable strictness and hostility. Within just two days, we realized there was no wedding—our parents had deceived us to bring us to Pakistan.

When we confronted Mother, she sided with Father and said, 'You two have become too rebellious. You need to be disciplined.'

Father, along with our uncles and older male cousins, would spend entire days secretly discussing something. Five days passed like this, and then Laiza finally confronted them, saying, 'You lied to us! I need to go back—I'm missing my studies.'

In response, Father slapped Laiza hard. Since I was standing nearby, he hit me too, though I hadn't said anything. Tears streamed down our faces as we stared at him in shock. He mockingly said with venom in his voice, 'Go ahead! Call 911 now!'

Then, he took out our passports, ripped them into pieces in front of us, and flung the scraps at our faces, shouting, 'Get out of my sight!'

We locked ourselves in our room, crying for a long time. We were devastated, filled with anger and fear for our future. A few days later, I discovered that they had arranged Laiza's marriage to my elder uncle's son for the following Thursday.

Laiza had no idea. When I told her, she was horrified. Pale-faced, she stammered, 'What are you saying?!'

I assured her it was true—I had overheard Mother and Aunt discussing it. But that wasn't all—my own marriage had been arranged for next month, with Uncle Farhan's middle son.

Upon hearing this, Laiza gasped, "We are doomed."

Her initial shock quickly turned into rage, and she stormed up to Mother, demanding, "What is this?! This is tyranny! I will not accept a forced marriage."

Mother ignored her protests and stood by Father, defending his decision.

Laiza then went straight to Father's room. He was sitting in his chair, reading a newspaper.

Laiza fell to her knees, grabbing his feet, and pleaded, "Father, please forgive me! I will do whatever you say. I will wear an abaya, I will observe hijab, I will never talk to boys, I will stay home, I will even abandon my education and study online. Just please, take me back to Canada—don't force me into this marriage. Please don't condemn me to hell while I'm still alive."

She cried and begged, but she could not break his false ego or newly awakened sense of honour. She even attempted a hunger strike one day, but it was useless. Mother and Father remained indifferent, as if their hearts had been emptied of all love and compassion for us. It seemed like only hatred and cruelty remained.

On the day of Laiza's wedding, I sat with her in the afternoon. Suddenly, Father entered the room and addressed her, "There must be no disturbances during the wedding. What we have decided is best for you. Whether you like it or not, accept it. Follow our instructions, or the consequences will be dire. You will be solely responsible for what happens."

With that, he left. I looked at Laiza—she was completely silent, but I knew she had made up her mind.

When the time for the wedding ceremony arrived, she stood up before everyone, looked at the officiating cleric, and loudly declared, "These people have imprisoned me illegally. They destroyed my passport and are now forcing me into marriage!"

Gasps filled the room—everyone was stunned.

Uncle, furious, roared, "Laiza! What nonsense are you spouting?!"

Father glared at her with sheer rage.

The cleric (Qazi) became furious and turned to my father and uncle, saying, "Shame on you! Is this how a marriage is conducted? Do you have no fear of God? A guardian's consent is necessary for a virgin's marriage, but her own consent is even more important. If she is rejecting this union so strongly, then neither her guardian nor even her father has the right to force her into it. In Islam, a marriage conducted under coercion is invalid. Forcing a girl into marriage is a grave injustice!"

With those words, the Qazi and other people left.

" What my father did to Laiza afterward—I can barely find the strength to recount it. My heart bleeds as I recall it, and I am struggling to put it into words." Maiza stopped speaking, her eyes brimming with tears.

Faiza remained silent, unable to find words of comfort for her.

Summoning her strength again, Maiza continued, "First, my father locked Laiza in a room, forbidding anyone from seeing her. She remained confined for two days—starving, thirsty, pounding on the door, begging to be let out. But no one listened to her pleas.

I begged my mother repeatedly, 'Please, at least let me give her food and water!' But she responded coldly, 'I can't do anything. Talk to your father. He locked her in there, and no one but him has the authority to open that door or enter the room.'

I pleaded with my father, 'If you won't let her out, at least let me give her some food and water, for God's sake!' But he slapped me and snarled, 'Get out of here, or I'll make you suffer the same fate!'

I appealed to my uncle, my maternal uncle, and other family members, but no one listened.

The next day, I was in my room when I suddenly heard loud voices and frantic crying from outside. Alarmed, I rushed out to see chaos spreading through the house. I ran toward Laiza's room and found the door wide open, with people crowding inside.

Heart racing, I pushed through and saw Laiza lying motionless on the floor.

I screamed, "What happened to her?!"

One of my cousins turned to me and uttered those dreadful words: "She's dead."

For a moment, I refused to believe it. Trembling, I cautiously pulled the sheet off her face—and then let out a blood-curdling scream, breaking into uncontrollable sobs. She was truly gone.

I uncovered her face once more, kissed her forehead, and then noticed something on her lips—traces of foam. As I looked closer, even then, I could still see faint froth coming from her mouth.

My gaze shifted to a broken glass lying a short distance away on the floor.

Fury overtook me. I stood up and screamed, "You poisoned her! You killed her! You are murderers!"

Before I could say anything more, my uncle grabbed me and dragged me out of the room. My father and uncle then locked me in another room.

My father loomed over me, his voice menacing, "Stop talking nonsense! Laiza died a natural death. She had a heart attack."

Through my sobs, I shouted back, "You're lying! I saw the foam—"

I couldn't finish my sentence because my father slapped me so hard that I fell back onto the bed.

Then, he and my uncle locked the door from the outside and walked away.

"Faiza, they killed my sister—they poisoned her!" Maiza finally broke down, sobbing uncontrollably.

Faiza, devastated by the revelation, felt her own heart sink with sorrow.

Faiza struggled to find words that could comfort Maiza.

A few minutes later, Maiza wiped her tears with her scarf and said, "Then, in the dead of night, they secretly buried Laiza without any ceremony or acknowledgment and spread the news that she had suddenly died due to heart failure."

After keeping me locked up for a day, they finally let me out, but with countless restrictions—I was forbidden from using a phone, and I was not allowed to step outside the house.

Everyone there was utterly indifferent. When Laiza's close friend in Canada learned about it, she refused to believe the fabricated story. She reached out to the media, and the case was published in the newspaper, demanding an investigation, as it did not seem like a natural death but rather a murder.

Yet, despite her efforts, nothing happened.

In this country, countless young men and women are unjustly murdered every month in the name of so-called honour, but no one pays any attention. The perpetrators—often close family members—walk free without any consequences.

Parents fail in their responsibility to properly educate and nurture their children. They do not teach them about religion, instil strong morals, or even work on their own faith and character. They spend their lives engraving the love of this world into their children's minds, and then, all of a sudden, they impose Islam upon them. If their children resist and hesitate in immediately accepting this forced transformation or wish to live on their own terms, they are denied the right to life. They are slaughtered in cold blood, sacrificed at the altar of false honour and excessive pride.

Anyway, I had fallen into complete silence. I barely spoke to anyone. As I endured this suffocating environment for three weeks, one day, I overheard my mother talking to my aunt.

Mother said, "I think we should delay the wedding a little. Laiza's loss is still too fresh."

Aunt replied, "That's true, but I fear that Maiza might end up like Laiza."

Mother sighed, "Please, don't say that. My heart is already shattered. I'll make sure Maiza understands and won't pull any reckless stunts."

I couldn't sleep that entire night. My mind was consumed with horrifying thoughts. At times, I imagined myself rejecting the marriage like Laiza did, only for my father to strangle me with both hands until I died. Other times, I thought of going to the police, or fleeing to the Canadian embassy in Islamabad.

But I had no knowledge of the routes, no familiarity with the maps of this place. I had no money, no resources, and no means to escape.

The next morning, I managed to sleep for a short while, but soon woke up. My entire body burned with fever.

Two days later, when I started recovering, I made up my mind. I firmly resolved that I would not surrender my life to these people so easily. I would fight with every ounce of strength to stay alive.

I would ensure that Laiza's tragic, nameless, and helpless death would not be erased—I would bring her killers to justice.

Then, one morning, I made the decision to escape. Seizing the right moment, I quietly slipped out of the house.

I had no knowledge of the roads, no escape plan—I was simply fleeing from a suffocating life of fear.

When they couldn't find me in my room, the entire household began searching for me. I knew that if any of them caught me, my fate would be no different from Laiza's.

With my face hidden behind my scarf, I kept moving in a chosen direction, without caring where the path led. All I knew was that I had to get far away from this place—beyond their reach.

I had been walking for more than an hour. As I continued along a side road, I suddenly felt the presence of a car stopping behind me. My blood ran cold as I turned around—my uncle and his son, Javed, were stepping out.

They ordered me to stop, but the moment I saw them, I broke into a run.

Seeing this, they started chasing me. Without thinking, I sprinted across the road—so focused on escaping that I failed to notice an oncoming car. It nearly hit me, missing me by inches while honking furiously.

My uncle and cousin saw me crossing and shouted from the other side, "Stop right now, or we'll shoot you!"

But I kept running. After crossing the road, they followed in pursuit, scanning their surroundings.

Then, I darted into a narrow alley, which seemed to be a marketplace for livestock feed. Suddenly, I spotted a pickup truck with a trailer hitched behind it, loaded with hay.

At that point, my uncle and cousin had gotten dangerously close. I quickly climbed into the trailer and buried myself beneath the hay to remain unseen.

A few moments later, they arrived, looking around but failing to spot me. They continued searching elsewhere.

Before I could climb out of the trailer, the pickup started moving.

It turned off the side road and merged onto a small highway. My first instinct was to scream so the driver would stop and let me out. But then I thought—why not leave it to fate? Let it take me as far away as possible.

Perhaps I could cross the border into another country. Once there, I would either apply for political asylum or contact the Canadian embassy to find a way back to Canada.

I didn't even know which countries bordered Pakistan. Nonetheless, I wasn't sure whether I'd even be able to cross a border.

All I knew was that I needed to escape. Lost in these thoughts, with fears and uncertainties swirling in my mind, I drifted into sleep.

When I woke up, the trailer had stopped in a lush green field. I saw a man approaching it—your brother, Zordar. He had parked the pickup, probably to collect something nearby.

From then on, well… you know the rest.

She paused for a moment, then looked at Faiza and said, "I know that my father, uncle, and other relatives are searching for me. If they find me, they might shoot me on sight. But I refuse to die in nameless obscurity.

What crime have I committed? I am a human being—I have the right to live.

The horrors that befell my sister—I do not wish to see them happen to me.

Is this Islam? To oppress women, to abuse them, to impose one's will upon them? To deny them the right to express their desires, their choices? To raise the banner of false honour while trampling over their tears and blood? In my eyes, neither is this Islam, nor is it humanity.

Anyway, I am deeply sorry for the troubles I have caused your brother and your family. Because of me, you have faced unnecessary difficulties.

But once I escape this country—perhaps I will finally receive permission to live."

Faiza walked up to Maiza, placed a reassuring hand on her shoulder, and said, "Do not worry at all. My brother, Zordar, is a man of honour and courage. He has given you shelter and promised to help you—he will never go back on his word.

We, the tribal people, are willing to sacrifice our own lives to protect the dignity and safety of our guests.

Islam teaches us to respect and safeguard women, but due to ignorance and false pride, people distort its true image.

Now, you don't need to have any fears. I will personally speak to my brother. He will ensure that you are safely taken to your country's embassy in Islamabad.

For now, take care of yourself."

With that, she walked away.

"Brother, I need to talk to you."

"What is it, Faiza Khani?" Zordar asked, unloading supplies from the pickup.

"Not here—let's go somewhere else. This is a long discussion," Faiza insisted.

"Is everything alright?" Zordar asked, looking at her with concern.

"Give me two minutes—I'll go tell Mother that I need to visit the market for a few things so I'm going with you. I'll explain everything on the way." Saying this, she went inside and soon returned, now dressed in a burqa and veil. "Let's go, brother."

On their way, Faiza narrated Maiza's entire ordeal to Zordar, concluding, "We need to help her."

After listening, Zordar sighed deeply and said, "Yara, this is a painful story. But she shouldn't have run away from her home like this—it's not what respectable women do. I am an honourable man, but God forbid if she had fallen into the hands of some criminal, what would have happened to her?"

Faiza replied, "Brother, you're right. But think about what she was facing—what else could she have done? They would have killed her, just like they did her elder sister."

"Yes, that's true. But now, what should I do? I'm already troubled because of this situation. Taking her to Islamabad isn't easy, but I'm trying. Tell her to stay patient—I will take her there within a day or two."

The morning sun filtered through the wooden lattice of the Zordar's house, casting shifting patterns on the floor.

Zordar Khan stood by the door, his arms crossed, waiting for Faiza.

In the guest room, Maiza had sat quietly on a mattress, her expression distant, her fingers tracing invisible patterns on the worn fabric of her shawl.

Faiza stepped out of her room, her face pale, her movements sluggish.

"Brother…" she started, pressing her hand to her forehead.

Zordar raised an eyebrow. "You look like you haven't slept all night."

"I don't feel well," she admitted, sitting on the edge of a low stool.

"What's wrong?" He asked, concern flashing in his eyes.

"Maybe something I ate… or just the exhaustion," Faiza sighed, shaking her head.

Zordar exhaled sharply. He had planned for Faiza to accompany them to Islamabad—her presence would have made things easier.

"You can't travel like this," he finally said. "Ok, I'll take her alone."

Faiza frowned. "Are you sure? Won't it be risky?"

Zordar shrugged. "What's done is done. What can I do? She wants to leave, and I need to make sure she gets there safely."

Faiza then slowly entered into the guest room and explained the situation to Maiza.

Maiza glanced at Faiza. "I'm sorry. I know I've caused trouble."

"It's not your fault," Faiza replied softly, forcing a weak smile. "Just… be careful."

Arranging for a rented jeep, Zordar Khan set off with Maiza toward Islamabad. As soon as his vehicle reached the village's main square, they spotted armed men standing ahead, seemingly blocking the path.

Seated in the back, Maiza also saw the weapons through the windshield and immediately panicked. She assumed they were thugs sent by her father and uncle.

"They have guns! They… they will definitely kill me!" she said in a terrified voice.

Zordar Khan replied, "You don't need to panic. If they fire at you, I will take the bullets on my chest—I will not let any harm come to you."

"But they have guns—so many of them!" Maiza continued fearfully.

"So what? I have one too." Saying this, he pulled out a pistol hidden under his clothes and showed it to Maiza.

"But don't worry," he reassured her. "I recognize them now. They are Mehrab Khan and his men. We don't have good relations, but I will handle them."

Hearing this, Maiza felt a slight relief—it was evident that these were people from Zordar's village, not hitmen sent by her father or uncle.

"Zordar Khan, who is this woman?" Mehrab Khan demanded in a loud voice.

"She is my friend's sister. I'm taking her to Islamabad," Zordar answered.

Mehrab Khan laughed mockingly. "Save this fairy tale for someone else. An unknown woman, traveling alone with you on such a long journey? We know she's been staying at your house for days. You must have some illicit relationship with her. We will not tolerate this shamelessness in the village."

Maiza was enraged by these accusations. Before Zordar could say anything, she leaned forward and shouted angrily in English, "Shut up, you bloody rascal!!! Have you no shame? How dare you slander an honourable man?"

"Oh, look! She bites too—and in the language of foreigners!" Mehrab Khan sneered, smiling wickedly.

"You stay quiet—I am talking," Zordar murmured, gently urging Maiza to calm down.

Outside, Mehrab Khan issued a stern warning, "Zordar Khan, you cannot take this woman and leave silently. This matter will be decided in the village council (Jirga). Turn back now, or there will be bloodshed right here. Under no circumstances will we let you take her beyond this point."

Realizing that they would never allow him to leave without escalating into violence, Zordar said, "Fine, I'll take her back home."

He then turned the jeep around and drove back toward his house.

"Zarmina, where is Zordar?" His father entered the house, his tone filled with anger.

"Take a breath, sit down—I'll call him," she replied calmly. She then instructed one of her younger daughters, "Run and get your brother." Turning to another daughter, she said, "Quickly, go and prepare a cold drink for Father."

Zordar's father, still furious, said:

"What nonsense were Jameela and Noreen talking about? I just met some men from Mukarram Khan's side. They told me they want to raise this issue about that guest woman in the Jirga. Who is she, and why is she still here?"

At that moment, Zordar arrived.

Seeing him, his father burst into rage, "Who is this woman? What is her real story? She's clearly not the sister of your friend from Kabul. What is being talked about in the village?"

"I'll explain everything," Zordar replied, then briefly recounted the situation. "Father, she is a troubled woman—not a disgraceful one. I gave her shelter."

"But what will I tell the community and the Jirga members now? Didn't you think of your five younger sisters? If our family is defamed, who will marry them? Everyone will spit on us!" His father shouted in fury.

"I was taking her to Islamabad, but Mehrab blocked the way and refused to let us pass," Zordar explained.

"I don't understand why you got involved in this in the first place. I think I need to talk to Mukarram Khan (Mehrab Khan's father) and convince him not to escalate the matter. If this issue goes to the Jirga, it will be disastrous—our reputation will be ruined," his father said.

"But Father, I know she is an oppressed woman, and I have done nothing wrong. I merely gave her refuge (Panah)," Zordar insisted.

His father sighed deeply and said, "Refuge is something people can easily misinterpret—especially when it involves an unknown, foreign woman. You don't realize the gravity of the situation. If the Jirga is convened and the decision turns out the way Mukarram Khan's men want it to, not only will our honour be destroyed, but your own life will also be in danger."

"It's been so many days, and still no sign of Maiza. I don't know if the sky has swallowed her or the earth has devoured her," Maiza's father said angrily.

"I can't figure out where she suddenly disappeared to. We were so close to catching her, and then—she vanished," her uncle remarked.

"If she went to the police, we could face serious trouble," her maternal uncle added.

"I don't think she reached the police. It's been days now—if she had gone to them, they would have come for us by now," her uncle reasoned.

"Please, just find her. Who knows what condition my daughter is in? What if someone has caught her… No, no! Please go and bring her back!"

Maiza's mother pleaded anxiously.

Her father turned on her in rage, snapping, "Shut up! This is all your doing! I made a mistake—I should have finished her off along with Laiza. Having a rebellious and disgraceful daughter is worse than having no children at all. The elder one humiliated us before the entire community, and now the younger one has smeared our faces with shame and fled!"

"What can we do now?" her uncle asked. "We have searched all of Peshawar and even several smaller towns and villages nearby, but there's no trace of her."

"Father, listen to me—file a report with the police," Javed, his nephew, suggested.

"Are you insane?! Do you want our family's reputation dragged through police stations and courts?" his uncle scolded him.

"You don't understand," Javed insisted. "If she gets caught by the police and gives a statement against us, they will immediately file charges. That would be serious trouble for us. Think about it—if the police ask why we didn't report her missing for a whole week, what will we say? That's why I'm telling you—filing a report will protect us."

"I actually think Javed is right. We should file a report—it's in our best interest," her maternal uncle agreed.

"I think she's dead by now, or worse—she fell into the wrong hands, and they eventually got rid of her," Maiza's father remarked heartlessly.

"What kind of father are you?! Don't say that. Go find her!" Maiza's mother protested.

"Why shouldn't I say it? If she's dead, it's better—we'll be spared from disgrace. And stop crying. This is all your fault!" he lashed out at her.

"Fine! Blame me for everything. You act like a butcher who refuses to listen to anyone! You already killed one daughter, and now you're hunting the other down!" she fired back.

"Enough nonsense! If you don't shut up, I might deal with you first!" he roared, losing his temper completely.

Maiza's uncle stepped in to calm him. "Control yourself. Arguing and fighting won't solve anything. Sister-in-law, you should leave now. I'll talk to him."

After Maiza's mother left, his nephew Javed suggested, "Uncle, why don't you and Aunt just go back to Canada? We can handle the legal matters and other issues here. One problem has already been buried, and this second one will settle down soon."

Maiza's father, now speaking in a lower tone, responded, "You don't understand. Here, these things can be concealed, but if any of their friends in Canada have filed a case against us, then the courts and laws there will take it very seriously. They will investigate thoroughly. Returning there right now is too risky. At this point, staying here is our only option."

"Mukarram Khan, I have come to your place myself. I heard that your son, Mehrab Khan, has complaints against my son, Zordar," said Zordar's father, Zamurd Khan.

"Zamurd Khan, it is an honour that you have come here yourself. But what can I do? Mehrab says Zordar's actions were disgraceful and shameful. We also have mothers, sisters, and daughters in our village. Such things go against our family and tribal traditions," Mukarram Khan lamented.

Zordar felt a surge of anger at this accusation but remained silent, as the two elders were speaking.

His father, attempting to calm the situation, said, "Mukarram Khan, forget what has happened. Tell your son not to escalate matters. I give you my word that we will remove this girl from here by tomorrow."

"That's fine, Zamurd Khan, but Mehrab says that bringing a stranger, an outsider, into your home and then trying to remove her quietly is unacceptable. He claims she is an immoral woman who speaks a foreign language," Mukarram Khan added.

At this, Zordar could no longer stay silent. "Uncle Mukarram, forgive me, but you're speaking unfairly. She is not immoral—she is oppressed!" he retorted.

Zamurd Khan immediately scolded him, "Stay quiet, Zordar! When elders are speaking, you remain silent!"

Mukarram Khan glared and said, "Zamurd Khan, you must also forgive us. This matter will now be settled in the Jirga. Whatever defence Zordar wants to make for this woman, he will present it before the Jirga."

On the way back, Zamurd Khan said angrily, "Why did you need to speak out? I was carefully handling the situation, softening him."

Equally frustrated, Zordar replied, "That woman is under my protection. You know that anyone under my shelter is my responsibility—I must protect their honour and life. Uncle Mukarram was falsely accusing her with disgusting allegations!"

"Still, not everything can be solved through emotions alone. Diplomacy is necessary. Wisdom must be applied. I have told you a thousand times to get an education, but you refused. If you had studied, you would have gained some understanding of the world and how to handle matters," his father spoke with a mix of anger and disappointment.

"Will you keep reminding me of this for the rest of my life?!" Zordar snapped.

"Forget it. Let's go home and think about what to do. Mukarram Khan and his son won't back down without taking this to the Jirga. On the other hand, your aunt and your uncle's wife have already stirred up the entire family over the presence of this woman in our home. You've put us all in a tough spot," his father sighed.

The Jirga members sat in a circular formation, with the elders and senior figures positioned in the centre.

On one side sat Mukarram Khan and his supporters, while on the other were Zamurd Khan and Zordar Khan. Other villagers sat scattered around.

One of the elders turned to Mukarram Khan and said, "Present your complaint."

Mukarram Khan responded, "With your permission, I will ask my son, Mehrab Khan, to present the complaint, as he is a direct eyewitness to the matter."

Mehrab Khan then exaggerated the entire situation, adding embellishments to his story. In conclusion, he declared, "Bringing a strange, unrelated woman into one's home, keeping her there for days without any legitimate relationship, and then secretly trying to smuggle her out—it is shameless and immoral. This is against our tribal traditions. This disgraceful woman and sinful Zordar must be severely punished!"

The elders of the Jirga discussed among themselves and then asked Mehrab for evidence and witnesses.

He immediately presented four men who had been with him the day he stopped Zordar Khan in the town square while he was en-route to Islamabad.

Mehrab Khan continued, "If my testimony and the witnesses are not enough, ask Zordar's aunt and his uncle's wife. We originally learned about this matter from the women of his own household. His aunt and uncle's wife shared all the details with the family and the village."

Mehrab then recounted, word for word, everything that Jameela and Noreen had spread throughout the village and extended family.

After listening, the elders turned to Zordar Khan. "Is it true that this woman is not the sister of your friend from Kabul?" they asked.

Zordar hesitated before replying, "No, she is not the sister of my friend."

"Then why did you lie to your family?" one elder asked.

"The circumstances were such that I was forced to," Zordar replied, his head lowered.

"So, you brought this unrelated woman all the way from Peshawar to Landi Kotal alone?" another elder asked.

"Yes... No... I mean... I did not bring her—she came on her own," Zordar stammered, trying to clarify.

"She came on her own! Without your permission or knowledge, she travelled with you from Peshawar to Landi Kotal? And then, she chose to stay in your home of her own will? Fascinating," one elder remarked sarcastically.

"No, I gave her shelter myself. But she arrived in Landi Kotal on her own," Zordar quickly clarified.

Another elder added, "So, she did indeed stay in your home for several days without any legitimate relationship or bond with your family. When the matter became public, you rented a jeep and attempted to smuggle her out quietly."

"That's not true! The jeep was not for an escape—it was to take her safely to Islamabad," Zordar hastily explained.

"Kabul first, and then Islamabad! Why did you offer refuge to this strange woman?" an elder questioned.

"She is helpless! What was I supposed to do—leave her to be devoured by wild beasts?" Zordar retorted in frustration.

"So, the accusations levelled against you by Mehrab Khan and even your own female relatives—are they true?" another elder asked.

"I have already explained—I did everything solely to help her. My intentions were never wrong," Zordar replied firmly.

"Help! Your own character appears suspicious after everything you've done!" an elder declared.

"Enough," another elder interrupted. "The Jirga is adjourned until tomorrow. You may all leave now, except for the elders. We will deliberate further on this matter."

"What are you saying?!" Zordar's mother exclaimed in distress.

Zordar's father responded in a voice filled with concern, "I am saying what is evident. The way things are going, it seems the Jirga's decision will be against us. Our reputation will be ruined. Worse, I fear Zordar might receive severe punishment because of this woman."

"You're scaring me!" she said, her voice trembling.

"I am deeply worried myself. We might be exiled from the village. We will be disgraced beyond repair," he muttered, holding his head in despair.

"What will happen to our daughters? Faiza's wedding is planned for next year, and soon enough, the others will be of age too. What future will they have?" she said anxiously.

"Go ask that son of yours—whose mind was grazing in the fields when he decided to do all this! I kept telling you to educate him, but neither you nor he ever listened. Now look—the uneducated remains uneducated. He has no worldly understanding and no ability to navigatc situations wiscly. " Hc said angrily.

Zordar's mother was speechless and extremely worried.

"He didn't think about who this woman was or why he was entangling himself in this mess. Pray that Allah provides some way out, or else we will suffer great humiliation and hardship," he ranted in frustration.

"Faiza, why do I feel like there's tension in your home? Everyone seems anxious. Is it because those armed men stopped us from leaving the other day?" Maiza asked.

Faiza had come to bring Maiza food. Placing the tray on the table, she replied, "The truth is that Mehrab Khan has filed a case against my brother, and the matter is now being discussed in the Jirga. Today was the first meeting, and tomorrow is the second—it might be the final one. We are all deeply worried."

"Mehrab Khan—isn't he the same thug who blocked us in the town square?" Maiza asked.

Faiza nodded, and Maiza continued, "But what did he file the case on?"

"He has twisted the situation and presented it in a completely dishonest way. He is making disgusting accusations against my brother," Faiza said in frustration.

"Oh..." Maiza murmured. "What exactly is a Jirga?"

"You can think of it as a local court. Village elders and senior members listen to issues and resolve them. Honestly, it embarrasses me to say this, but that lying Mehrab Khan is accusing my brother of immoral acts and spreading indecency," Faiza replied.

"But that's all false!" Maiza protested.

"Of course, it's a blatant lie, but my parents were saying that the Jirga members are sceptical of my brother and aren't believing anything he says."

"Oh my God," Maiza exclaimed.

Faiza, her voice heavy with concern, added, "My father also said that if the Jirga rules against us, both my brother and you could be in danger. They might even expel us from the village."

"I am deeply sorry that my presence has brought such hardship upon your family. Is there anything I can do for you or especially for Zordar? Should I speak to them?" Maiza asked anxiously.

"Normally, the Jirga proceedings involve only men. Women are not included. However, in rare cases, the elders might listen to a woman's statement from behind a screen (purdah). For now, just pray to Allah that the decision is made in our favour," Faiza said worriedly.

"Javed, son, hurry and go get your father! Your uncle's condition has worsened!" Maiza's mother cried out frantically.

A short while later, Maiza's uncle, her mother's brother, and their sons arrived. Seeing them, Maiza's mother said, "Come quickly! He's talking in a delirious manner!"

As they entered the room, Maiza's father blurted out, "I am a murderer… I killed my elder daughter… then I killed my younger daughter too… Ha ha ha ha… I am a murderer!"

"Bhai, are you in your senses?" His brother asked.

"Who are you people?! How did you enter my room without my permission?" he shouted, behaving like a man who had lost his mind.

"Uncle, what has happened? Don't you recognize us?" Hassan, the younger son of his brother, asked.

"Who are you?! Who is this insolent fool questioning me? Throw him out of here!" he screamed wildly.

"Brother, I think uncle has lost his mental balance," Hassan whispered to cousin, Javed.

"Get out of here, all of you! I am a murderer… I am a murderer!" he repeated, walking in circles around the room.

Seeing this, his brother said, "Sister, it seems something has affected his mind. He must be taken to the doctor immediately."

"I'm not going to any doctor! I am perfectly fine!" Maiza's father snapped.

"I agree—he must be taken to the hospital immediately," Maiza's uncle said.

"Oh, so you'll take me to the hospital? Let me send you to the graveyard right now!" he suddenly lunged at his brother in a fit of madness, grabbing his throat and choking him.

His nephews quickly rushed forward—one of them pulled their father free while the other restrained Maiza's father, tying his hands to prevent him from hurting anyone or himself.

"Get him to the hospital—quickly!" his brother shouted.

Coughing, Maiza's uncle agreed. "Yes, hurry, before he harms himself or anyone else!"

They forcibly placed him in the car and sped toward the hospital.

"When that woman didn't have proper documents, why did you take her toward Kabul?" one of the Jirga elders asked.

"I didn't know. She told me on the way that she had no identification papers," Zordar Khan responded.

"So you took her with you without confirming such an important detail? Alright, what happened next?" another elder asked.

"Then she told me to take her to Islamabad," Zordar replied.

"Islamabad? Why?" the elder questioned.

"Actually, there is a country called Ka-ne-da in Islamabad. She wanted to go there," Zordar said.

The elder, lowering his tone, asked, "Do you mean she wanted to go to the Canadian embassy in Islamabad? Why?"

"Yes...yes, that's exactly what I mean. She is a citizen there," Zordar clarified.

Upon hearing this, the elder reacted sharply, saying, "Oh… so now we've learned that this girl isn't Pakistani—she is a Canadian citizen. This could mean that she is a foreign spy, using you to conduct espionage here."

Mehrab Khan and his men rejoiced at this revelation—surely the Jirga would not spare Zordar Khan now. Espionage was considered one of the most serious crimes. The accusations against Zordar were already grave, and this new suspicion only strengthened their case.

Meanwhile, Zordar Khan sensed that he was on the verge of being declared guilty and that the verdict against him was imminent.

The elders engaged in a discussion among themselves when suddenly, a boy approached one of the senior Jirga members with a message. The elder reacted with surprise, saying, "What does she want to say?"

After thinking for a moment, he turned to the other elders and said, "I believe we should hear this woman's statement as well."

Some of the elders agreed, but most opposed, stating that the situation was clear and there was no need for her testimony. However, the senior elder insisted, "No, the allegations against her are extremely serious, and the punishment could be severe. It is essential that we hear what she has to say and not rush to a decision."

The Jirga then ordered arrangements for a covered space to be made so that the woman could present her statement.

Within a short time, a small enclosure was created using thick sheets, and Maiza was called inside, seated behind the barrier.

One of the elders began speaking to her from behind the veil.

"What is your full name? According to Zordar Khan, you ran away from your home. Why? And why are you with Zordar Khan?" the elder asked many questions.

"My name is Maiza Khan. I am a Canadian citizen of Pakistani descent. My parents originally lived in a town near Peshawar. I was born in Canada. I had one sister, and we both grew up in Canada.

Later, my father deceived us, bringing us to Pakistan and trying to forcibly marry us to his brother's and brother-in-law's sons. When my sister refused, they murdered her.

I feared they would kill me next, so I escaped from home.

Eventually, I ended up here. In this entire situation, Zordar Khan has no fault. He had no idea that I was hiding in his trailer, which was attached to his pickup, as I fled for my life from my family.

That's how I travelled from Peshawar to here.

When he first saw me, he was shocked and immediately told me to leave. I did leave his farmland, but by then, darkness had already set in.

Out of mercy, he gave me shelter and brought me to his home."

"What proof do you have that what you are saying is true?" the elder asked.

"Please look at this," Maiza said, extending a newspaper clipping through the veil—one that Faiza had given her.

She continued, "This is my sister Laiza's picture, along with the news article about her. If you need further proof, you can contact the Canadian embassy and verify our entire record. I don't have a passport because my father tore it apart and discarded it after we arrived in Pakistan," she explained.

The elder then left to consult with the other senior Jirga members. After deliberating for a while, he returned and asked Maiza, "Girl, tell the truth—what is your relationship with Zordar Khan? If there is something between you two, admit it clearly. We will show leniency. But if you lie, there will be no mercy."

Maiza responded, "I will not speak about my own character, but I am willing to swear any oath to defend Zordar Khan's honour. I testify before God that he is an upright and honourable man.

I have no relationship with him other than that he saw me as helpless and oppressed and offered his protection.

If his act of kindness is such a grave sin, then please erase the word 'humanity' from every language.

If you must punish someone, then punish me—because if anyone should be held responsible for all of this, it is me. I ran for my life and, in doing so, became a burden on others.

Punish me!

When I fled my home, I was consumed by the fear of death.

But after staying here for a few days, that fear has completely left me.

I am no longer afraid—neither of death nor of those who wish to kill me.

If you do not believe my words, then by all means, sentence me. But let this innocent man go free."

Hearing this, the elder replied, "We do not punish anyone deliberately, nor do we neglect justice. Tell your full story from the beginning in complete detail. The Jirga wants to understand—if you are truly innocent, how did you end up in this situation?"

Maiza then narrated everything from the beginning.

In the end, she said, "My father and relatives murdered my innocent sister in the name of false honour and pride.

You now have the choice to endorse yet another fabricated falsehood and punish me alongside an honourable man.

Tell me—what difference would there be between you and my oppressive family?

Am I not a Muslim woman?

Are you not Muslims?

Is this not an Islamic state?

Is there no shelter for a vulnerable and forsaken woman here?

If there isn't, then for God's sake, send me back to Canada.

Even if they are disbelievers, I am sure they will give me justice.

They will offer me protection."

Maiza was crying, speaking emotionally, her voice echoing with desperation.

Her story and words left the Jirga elders and other senior figures in stunned silence.

For several moments, no one uttered a single word.

Then, they began deliberating among themselves.

One of the senior elders of the Jirga turned to Maiza and said, "Daughter, you will receive justice and protection from the Muslims—that is your right. You do not need to seek justice at the doors of foreign nations. This Jirga has concluded that you have indeed suffered great injustice and that you are completely innocent. Zordar Khan is also a man of honour and free of any wrongdoing.

Before we discuss your case further, the Jirga will first address Mukarram Khan and his son."

Turning toward Mukarram Khan's group, the elder declared:

"Mukarram Khan, Mehrab Khan, and their associates—the Jirga strongly warns you against suspicion and baseless accusations. If any of you engage in such disgraceful and irresponsible behaviour again, not only will you receive public lashings, but your testimony will never be accepted again, and your family will be exiled from the village."

"The same warning applies to the women of Zamurd Khan's family who indulge in gossip, slander, and malicious rumours."

"The Jirga now orders Mehrab Khan to publicly apologize to Zordar Khan in front of everyone."

After that turning back to Maiza, the elder continued:

"Maiza, daughter, from today, you are the daughter of this village—our honour.

If you wish to go to Islamabad, we will escort you there with full protection and dignity.

If you wish to stay here, then know that the entire village is yours. From now on, no one will dare to raise their eyes toward you.

And as for your father and relatives—do not fear them.

This is not Peshawar. This is a village in Landi Kotal. Here, your family cannot harm you.

If you wish, you may forgive your family.

If not, tell us—this Jirga can request the Political Agent of Khyber Agency to file charges against them in Peshawar and ensure legal proceedings are carried out.

The Jirga deeply regrets the suffering you and your sister endured. Typically, the people of Peshawar are known to be educated, religious, and wise. Unfortunately, a few ignorant individuals tarnish the reputation of all."

Upon arriving home, Faiza embraced Maiza with joy, saying, "Congratulations! Thank God the Jirga ruled in our favour and cleared both you and my brother with dignity."

Maiza, equally happy, replied, "Yes, today, I feel truly joyful—not because my life was spared, but for two reasons."

"Oh? And what are those reasons?" Faiza asked with a smile.

"First, because the Jirga acquitted Zordar. If he had been punished despite being innocent, I would never have been able to forgive myself.

And second, because coming here has taught me what true honor is… what it means to respect women… what Islam truly represents.

This world is not filled with angels; there are good people, and there are bad.

But in the simplicity of this place, I have seen honesty, Islam, and humanity."

Maiza spoke passionately, her eyes brimming with tears.

Faiza smiled and said:

"Alhamdulillah, this is truly a blessing. We are all so relieved! Now, tell me, what is your plan? Will you stay with us, or do you still want to go to Islamabad? Honestly, we all wish you would stay."

Maiza smiled gently and replied:

,"I have already caused enough trouble for you all. I think I will go to Islamabad, get a new passport from the embassy, and return to Canada. "

" Oh !!! "

Faiza sadly uttered.

Maiza continued, " I have forgiven my parents and relatives—I do not wish to take any legal action against them. But I cannot return to them, nor will they ever accept me.

I have realized that when a girl runs away from home, it becomes a stain that can never be erased—no matter how many times she tries to justify herself. In such circumstances, the best choice is to go far away."

Faiza held Maiza's hand and said, "First of all, you have not troubled us—you were merely a victim of circumstances.

Secondly, we are honoured to host you. Now that the Jirga has granted you permission to stay here, I don't think traveling alone back to Canada is wise.

How will you manage all by yourself there? Please stay with us. It would bring us great happiness!"

Maiza replied with a soft smile, "You are very kind, but I think returning is best for me."

"Brother, where are you? I've been looking all over the house!" Faiza called out.

"I'm here, Faiza Khani. Come in. What's the matter?" Zordar Khan replied, seated in a quiet corner of the house.

"Brother, I spoke to Maiza. She wants to return to Canada and go to Islamabad first," Faiza said, sitting on a nearby chair.

"So what am I supposed to do?" Zordar Khan said in frustration.

"What do you mean?! Brother, you need to take her to Islamabad and arrange for her journey!" Faiza exclaimed in disbelief.

"Fine, I will do it. Just ask her when she wants to leave," Zordar said.

"Brother, look at me," Faiza said, gazing at him.

But Zordar turned his face further away and said, "I told you—I will arrange everything. Just go ask her and tell me the date."

Faiza looked at him meaningfully and said, "Brother, doesn't it matter to you that she's leaving?"

"Why should it matter to me? If she wants to go, let her go. What can I do?" Zordar replied.

"Then why are your eyes teary?" Faiza asked, looking directly at him.

"You foolish girl… Why would I cry? Now, just go and tell her to prepare," Zordar scolded her, still refusing to turn his face toward her.

Faiza sighed and said, "Brother, you don't want her to leave, do you? Why don't you just say it?"

"I am an uneducated tribal man… And she is an educated woman from Ka-ne-da… What connection do we have? Even if I spoke, what would I say? And why would she stay here? Besides, what does this place even have to offer her?"

Zordar said in a defeated tone.

"Brother, just say it once—maybe she will agree," Faiza suggested.

"It won't make a difference," Zordar said in a distant voice.

"Shall I ask her on your behalf?" Faiza offered.

"No, Faiza Khani, just leave it be. Don't say anything. Now, go," Zordar replied.

"Brother, have you placed all the luggage in the jeep?" Faiza asked.

"Yes, it's done. Now bring her out. I'll wait outside," Zordar Khan replied.

"Alright, brother, I'll bring her now," Faiza said before heading inside to the guest room, where Maiza was already prepared.

Faiza said, "All your belongings have been loaded into the jeep. If you're ready, shall we go?"

"My belongings? What belongings?" Maiza asked in surprise.

"Mother has given you some outfits and gifts. I packed everything into a bag and placed it in the jeep," Faiza explained.

"Oh! Thank you so much. I visited your mother, but she didn't mention anything about these gifts. You people are incredibly kind and hospitable," Maiza said gratefully.

"It's just a small gesture. Please don't embarrass us by thanking us too much. Anyway, if you're ready, shall we go?" Faiza asked.

"Yes, let's go. But tell me, is it possible to have one last conversation with your brother before we leave?" Maiza asked.

"Of course. Just stand behind the curtain near the door, and I'll call my brother. He'll stand outside, and you can speak to him from behind the veil," Faiza suggested before stepping outside to call Zordar.

A short while later, Zordar Khan's voice came from outside. "I'm here. What do you want to say?"

Maiza spoke softly, "Before I leave, I want to thank you. I will never be able to forget your kindness.

And secondly, I want to apologize for the troubles and difficulties my presence has caused you and your family."

"It's alright. It was my duty," Zordar Khan replied.

"In these few weeks, I have learned life lessons I could never have grasped in all my years in Canada.

In this tribal setting and its simplicity, I have understood what true sincerity is, what courage means, what honor for women looks like, and how one upholds their word.

I am deeply grateful to you," Maiza said.

"Thank you too. I am happy that I was able to be of some help to you," Zordar Khan replied from outside.

Maiza said, "Today, hearing you in a soft tone feels unusual—but it's nice."

"Anyway, I have something to return to you—or rather, something that belongs to you."

"What is it?" Zordar Khan asked curiously.

"Your shawl," Maiza said, extending it out through the door. You gave it to me the first time we met—to cover myself."

"But it's yours now. I won't take it back," Zordar Khan refused to accept it.

Faiza was nearby, listening to their conversation. She stepped in, smilingly saying, "You two won't resolve this on your own. I'll have to do something."

She took Zordar's hand and led him aside.

"Brother, I spoke to Mother, and she asked Father. They would both be very happy if Maiza married you. Do you have any objections to this wedding?" She said.

Shyly, Zordar replied, "I have no objections. But why would she agree to marry someone like me—an uneducated man?"

"Leave that to me. You stay here, I'll go speak to Maiza," Faiza said.

Inside, Faiza approached Maiza.

"Maiza, I have a request. But please think about it carefully before answering." Faiza said.

Maiza looked at her in surprise. "Yes, tell me. What is it?"

"Would you consider not going to Islamabad and staying here instead?" Faiza asked.

"But how would that be possible?" Maiza replied.

"It would be possible if you accept our proposal," Faiza said with a smile.

"Proposal? What proposal?" Maiza asked in confusion.

"My brother wants to marry you. Mother and Father also desire this, and I sincerely hope for it. But there is no pressure or coercion on you. Take your time, think it over, and then give us your answer," Faiza said, making playful gestures with her hands and mouth, urging her to agree.

Seeing Faiza's excitement, Maiza smiled and replied, "We come from different worlds. Our environments are vastly different.

If I say yes, I fear that these cultural differences could create cracks in our relationship down the line.

But at the same time, something inside me tells me that when there is love, respect and sincerity, all obstacles are nothing more than walls of sand.

The outwardly free and beautiful atmosphere of the West is, in truth, deeply materialistic and unforgiving.

The simplicity, sincerity, and love here are far greater than what that world offers.

I have no objections to this marriage—in fact, it would be my good fortune. Because I now understand that a woman needs love, respect, and security to live.

And I have full hope and confidence that I will find that here.

But I have one condition."

"A condition?! What condition?" Faiza asked anxiously.

Her face, which had lit up with joy upon hearing Maiza's agreement, suddenly fell at the mention of a condition.

"The condition is that Zordar must promise me that after marriage, I will teach him to read and write," Maiza said with a laugh.

Before Faiza could respond, they heard loud coughing from outside.

Faiza smirked and said, "I'll be back in a second."

She stepped outside, her face beaming with excitement, and turned to Zordar Khan.

"Brother, congratulations! She has agreed—but she has one condition."

"Pardon me, but I heard everything. Tell her—I accept her condition," Zordar Khan said joyfully.

Faiza smiled and said, "Then start unloading the luggage from the jeep!"

She then went inside, kissed Maiza on the forehead, and said with joy, "Brother accepts your condition."

THE END.

ABOUT THE AUTHOR

Writing under the pen name Aakh , the author is an electrical engineer by profession, working in the oil & gas sector for the past twenty five years. A Canadian citizen of Pakistani origin, he nurtured a lifelong love of writing that began as a quiet hobby—and has now found form in English through adaptations of stories originally penned in Urdu. When not immersed in words, he finds joy in exploring new places and reading deeply.

ALPHABETICAL GLOSSARY OF URDU TERMS IN PANAH

- Abaya – A long, loose-fitting outer garment worn by Muslim women for modesty.
- Amaan – Peace.
- Assalam o Alaikum – Islamic greeting meaning "Peace be upon you."
- Burqa – A full-body cloak worn by some Muslim women, including a face covering with mesh screen.
- Hijab – A headscarf worn by many Muslim women as a symbol of modesty and faith.
- Jirga – Traditional tribal council used to settle disputes.
- Khan Sahib – A respectful title for a man, akin to "Mr. Khan" or "Sir."
- Khala – Maternal aunt (mother's sister).
- Khani – Honorific used for women, similar to "Miss" or "Lady."
- Khocha – Rustic or informal address for someone, akin to "mister" or "you," sometimes gruff.
- Landi Kotal – A town near the Afghan border in Pakistan, known for tribal culture.
- Maghrib prayer – Islamic evening prayer performed just after sunset.
- Nikah – Islamic marriage contract.

- Non-mehram – A person of the opposite gender whom one could lawfully marry (i.e., not a close relative).
- Panah – Refuge or sanctuary.
- Paratha – Layered, pan-fried flatbread commonly eaten in South Asia.
- Pathan – Ethnic Pashtuns, known for their tribal values, courage, and hospitality; also associated with strong adherence to tradition.
- Peshawar – A historic city in northwest Pakistan, central to Pashtun culture.
- Phuppi – Paternal aunt (father's sister).
- Purdah – Practice of veiling or maintaining modesty, often for women.
- Qazi – An Islamic judge who officiates matters like marriage and divorce.
- Shaal – Shawl used for warmth or modesty.
- Torkham – Major border crossing between Pakistan and Afghanistan.
- Yara – Informal word for "friend" or "buddy," used warmly or playfully.

A REFUGE FOUND, A TRUTH UNVEILED

Panah is not merely the story of one girl's escape—it is a testament to survival, resilience, and the unwavering pursuit of justice. Maiza's journey is more than an act of defiance; it is a fight for dignity, the rejection of oppressive traditions, and the reclamation of her own life.

Through her struggles, we are reminded that:

- Honour lies in humanity, not control.
- Fear is a cage, but courage breaks chains.
- Hospitality and kindness transcend borders.
- Parents should nurture their children with love, guidance, and moral values, leading by example to inspire faith rather than imposing it.
- Justice demands voices that refuse to be silenced.

In the end, Panah is not just about finding refuge—it is about discovering the strength to fight back, the will to survive, and the hope that, even in the darkest of circumstances, change is possible.

UPCOMING NOVELS BY AAKH

Step into a world where the quiet strength of resilience, the weight of moral choice, and the silent currents of revolution intertwine. These forthcoming novels illuminate the human journey—not just in moments of triumph or tragedy, but in the nuanced spaces in between. Through evocative storytelling, the author explores the fragile, luminous balance between shadow and light that defines the essence of our shared experience.

Beyond the inner landscapes of individual resilience, the author's forthcoming novels delve into the intricate web of relationships and the delicate tensions between tradition and modernity. Through vivid characters and immersive storytelling, these works navigate pressing social issues, celebrate the guiding light of religious practice, and examine the powerful influence of upbringing in shaping ethical, compassionate citizens. Woven into the narratives are echoes of political triumphs and moral reckonings—each story a tribute to the tireless pursuit of a more just, secure, and thriving society.

1. Panah (Refuge)
2. Baaghi (The Rebellion)
3. If & But : Logically Ever After
4. Romziana: Where the Wind Folds Light
5. A Whisper of Relief
6. Do or Die
7. Verbal Gymnastics
8. Restlessness
9. Kind Strangers
10. Unfinished Dreams

11. Colorless Rainbow
12. Solace
13. The cursed one
14. Atonement
15. Mr. Ignoramus
16. Hero Zero
17. Benevolence
18. Hidden in Plain Light
19. One Life Isn't Enough
20. Retribution
21. Nawab Sahib (Not-So-His-Highness)

www.ingramcontent.com/pod-product-compliance
Lightning Source LLC
Chambersburg PA
CBHW041300210926
51847CB00009B/94
9789698592561